Mystery Pups

MISSING!

Mystery
Pups

MISSING!

by Jodie Mellor
Illustrated by Penny Dann

SIMON AND SCHUSTER

SIMON AND SCHUSTER
First published in Great Britain in 2009 by Simon and Schuster UK Ltd
A CBS COMPANY

Text copyright © 2009 Jenny Oldfield
Illustrations copyright © 2009 Penny Dann
Cover illustration copyright © 2009 John Butler

The right of Jenny Oldfield to be identified as the author of this work and of Penny Dann
and John Butler to be identified as the respective interior and cover illustrators of this work
has been asserted by them in accordance with sections 77 and 78 of the Copyright,
Designs and Patents Act, 1988.

Simon & Schuster UK Ltd
1st Floor, 222 Gray's Inn Road, London WC1X 8HB.

This book is a work of fiction. Names, characters, places and incidents are either the
product of the author's imagination or are used fictitiously. Any resemblance to actual
people living or dead, events or locales is entirely coincidental.

A CIP catalogue record for this book is available from the British Library.

ISBN: 978-1-84738-226-9

Printed and bound in Great Britain
by CPI Cox and Wyman, Reading, Berkshire RG1 8EX

www.simonsays.co.uk

CHAPTER ONE

"I can't wait to get back to Sleuth City," Lauren said, sitting with her puppy, Buster, on the grass in her friend Megan's garden. "It's the only place where exciting things happen!"

Megan brushed her own puppy's sleek black coat. Dylan sat perfectly still beside her with his eyes half closed in pleasure. "We have to wait for Caitlin and Daisy," Megan reminded her friend.

"Sleuth City is so cool!" Lauren sighed dreamily, then gave Buster a hug. "The man at Magic Mountain Rescue Centre *told* us that our puppies were special."

"But not *how* special!" Megan grinned.

"Magic-special!"

"Super-special!"

"Like no other puppies in the whole world!" Lauren tickled Buster's tummy.

Buster rolled, then jumped up. *Yap!* He ran up and down the long lawn with Dylan close behind.

"Hurry up, Caitlin!" Lauren went to the garden gate to look along the street. "What's keeping her? This is Saturday - Puppy Club day!"

Just then she saw Caitlin turn the corner with her little toy dog, Daisy, tucked under her arm. "Here she comes!"

Megan joined Lauren at the gate. Caitlin was walking slowly with her head down. "What's up with her?" she wondered.

"What's wrong?" Lauren asked, running down the street to meet Caitlin.

"Oh hi, Lauren. Nothing's wrong."

"You look sad," Megan said, as she held the gate open. Their friend's face was pale, her long,

golden-red hair loose around her shoulders.

"And you should be happy," Lauren insisted, letting lively Buster jump up at her as she came back into the garden. "Today's Saturday!"

"Today we get to go back to Sleuth City – we hope!" Megan picked Dylan up and let him say hi to Daisy. "I've got Dylan's medallion in my pocket."

"And I've got Buster's!" Lauren pulled the medal out of her pocket and let it dangle on its

7

bright red ribbon. Buster pricked up his ears and yelped. "How about you, Caitlin? Have you brought Daisy's medallion and your badge?"

Caitlin nodded. "Sorry I'm late," she muttered. "Mum took me up to Magic Mountain Rescue Centre. We only just got back."

Lauren and Megan gasped.

"Say that again!" Lauren cried. "Your mum took you to Magic Mountain? Wow!"

"To get you a puppy?" Megan asked. "A real live puppy?"

"Hush!" Covering Daisy's ears, Caitlin nodded. "Mum feels sorry for me 'cos you two have got Dylan and Buster and I've only got Daisy. She said I could choose a dog and bring it home."

"So why aren't you grinning and laughing and jumping up and down like a crazy person?" Lauren demanded. "Isn't that what you've always wanted?"

"Did you choose a puppy?" Megan asked

8

more quietly.

"Not yet. The man at Magic Mountain said I should take my time, not rush into things. We just had a look then came away again."

"I don't get it." Lauren frowned, picking Buster up. The three girls stood in a small circle in the middle of the lawn. "If it had been me, I'd have chosen the cutest one and brought it home right away!"

"But Caitlin's *not* you," Megan pointed out. She thought she understood Caitlin's problem. 'You're thinking about Daisy, aren't you?"

Caitlin sighed and nodded. "Sshh, I don't want her to hear! I really want a live puppy, but Daisy will be jealous if I get one. I know she will."

"But Daisy's not real. She's a toy," Lauren pointed out.

"Not in Sleuth City," Megan said. In Sleuth City Daisy was as alive as Dylan and Buster – a silky little Yorkshire terrier hot on the trail of

9

dognappers and art thieves.

"Ah!" Lauren realised.

"Exactly!" Caitlin said, setting Daisy down on the grass and taking out her medallion. "Anyway, let's not talk about it any more in front of Daisy. Let's put our badges on and say our Puppy Club promises."

"Yes, let's do it!" Lauren agreed. "Sleuth City, here we come!"

"Sit!" Megan told Dylan.

The little black Labrador sat with his ears pricked and his brown eyes shining.

"Sit, Buster!" Lauren said.

The creamy mongrel pup fidgeted and panted beside Dylan.

"Sit!" Caitlin popped Daisy down beside Dylan and Buster. Daisy's eyes stared blankly back.

Megan, Lauren and Caitlin put on their badges. They knew the Puppy Club promises off by heart.

"We promise to look after our puppies well. We promise to train them properly. We promise to feed them and play with them…"

"Ready?" Megan asked.

Lauren and Caitlin nodded and leaned forward. Together they hung the three gold medallions around their puppies' necks.

"Whoa!" Straight away Megan felt dizzy. She put her hands on the ground to steady herself.

"Whoo!" Lauren cried. "Here we go!" She was floating through the air, beginning to spin round and round with Buster beside her.

Caitlin saw Daisy's medallion glitter in the sun. She gasped as Daisy blinked and twitched her ears. "Hold on, wait for us!" she cried as they all whirled upwards into a dazzling white light.

And the three girls and their magic puppies spun high into the air, until Megan's garden looked tiny and her street stretched away like a grey ribbon into the green, blurred distance below.

CHAPTER TWO

"Oh!" Lauren looked around in surprise. She was sitting on smooth grass. Birds were chirping in the nearby trees. "Did that work? Where are we?"

"It doesn't feel as if we're in Sleuth City, that's for sure." Caitlin waited for her head to stop spinning, then looked around for tall buildings and busy streets. All she saw instead was a big lake and lawns criss-crossed by neat paths.

"We're in an enormous park," Megan announced. She watched Dylan, Buster and Daisy run off to play with other dogs whose owners jogged by in sweatshirts and trainers, ears plugged in to their favourite music. "Come back, Dylan!" she ordered.

Her magic pup had jumped up at a jogger wearing sunglasses and carrying a lightweight rucksack as he ran purposefully towards the wide exit gates onto the main street.

"Huh." Lauren was disappointed. "I was expecting action, not snoozing in a park on a sunny afternoon."

Reluctantly, Dylan obeyed Megan's command and trotted back towards her.

An old woman sitting on a bench looked up from her book and yelled at Lauren. "Hey, kid, control your dog. It's hassling me."

"He's only having a good sniff," Lauren explained.

"Yeah, and I'm trying to read." The grumpy, frizzy-haired woman turned her back.

"Oops, Buster, we're in trouble – already!" Picking him up, Lauren rejoined Megan and Caitlin. "At least Daisy came back to life," she grinned. "That's one good thing."

"And I don't think she heard us talking about the P U P P Y!" Caitlin said carefully. "Has anyone got a scrunchie? I want to tie my hair back. Hey, stay down, Daisy. I'll stroke you when I've done my hair."

Little Daisy jumped and yapped for joy. She ran round in circles then rolled on her back.

"So?" Caitlin wondered, fixing her hair then taking in their surroundings. "You're right, Megan – this park is huge. But look, you can see skyscrapers at the far side of the lake, and some glitzy shops behind us. So I guess we're right in the middle of Sleuth City after all."

"But why *here*?" Lauren demanded. People sunbathed on the grass. Roller-bladers glided along the paths. "It's Snoozeville."

"No crimes for the pups to solve," Caitlin

agreed. Just ice-cream stalls and women wheeling pushchairs.

"Come here, Buster!" Lauren had taken her eye off her pup for one second and he'd sprinted off towards the lake. Ducks were quacking and flying up in all directions.

"Shall we get you an ice-cream?" Megan called after her.

"Yes, please. Chocolate-chip and mint flavour!" And off Lauren sprinted.

"Mango and peach for me," Caitlin decided as she and Megan joined the queue.

"That's one chocolate-chip and mint, one mango and peach and one strawberry and vanilla," Megan told the man behind the stall.

"Daisy, come here!" Caitlin turned to see that her pup had raced after Buster and Lauren, leaping over the bench where the frizzy-haired woman sat. "Come back!" she cried, sprinting after Daisy.

"Which leaves me with three giant ice-creams

melting in the sun …" Megan sighed. She turned round to look for Dylan. "Hey!" she yelled, as her dog disappeared too. "Dylan, come back here this minute!"

"I don't know what got into them." Lauren had grabbed hold of Dylan's collar and held on to him until Megan joined them. "They just sprinted off without any warning."

"I know." Megan was out of breath as she handed the dripping ice-cream cones to Lauren and Caitlin. "Dylan never disobeys orders.

I mean, never!"

"Do you think they were trying to tell something?" Caitlin asked. She licked her ice-cream while keeping a firm hold of Daisy. Lauren had caught up with Buster just as he'd reached the side of the lake. There was a flurry of beating wings and angry quacks as ducks flew up into the air, then landed again with a skid and a splash on the smooth water. "Probably. But what?" Gazing round the vast park, Lauren wished, not for the first time, that the magic pups could talk. "I can't see anything wrong, can you?"

"Everything looks completely boring and normal," Megan agreed.

"What is it, Daisy?" Caitlin asked. She picked up her pup and stared hard into her Yorkie's sparkling brown eyes.

"Yip! Yip!" Daisy's bark was high-pitched and excited.

"Do you want to show me?"

"Yip!"

So Caitlin put Daisy back down on the ground and let her run on around the edge of the lake.

"Yap, yap!" Buster and Dylan were eager to follow.

"But don't trip people up!" Megan warned.

"Or chase any more ducks," Lauren added.

The girls ran hard to keep up with the pups – to the far side of the lake, past a café crowded with customers at outside tables and along a path designed for joggers, the quickest way to exit the park.

"Watch out!" A girl in a white T-shirt and running shoes almost stumbled over Dylan and went sprawling.

"Sorry!" Megan mumbled. She and the others wove their way towards the wide gates.

"Keep those dogs on a leash!" a man told the girls. It was the jogger with the rucksack who they'd seen earlier, but now he was minus his sunglasses. And this time he was sprinting rather than jogging.

"Sorry!" Caitlin and Lauren stammered as Daisy and Buster jumped up at him. "Come here, you naughty dogs!" they cried, grabbing their pups while the bad-tempered runner sprinted on.

And then suddenly the silence of the afternoon was broken by the wail of police sirens on the wide road that ran by the park. *Waah-waah, waah-waah!*

Lauren's eyes lit up. There were three white police cars, sirens wailing, screeching to a halt at the foot of a tall building. Officers jumped out, leaving the orange lights flashing. "Cool!" she gasped, dashing out of the park after Buster.

"Yip!" Daisy wriggled in Caitlin's arms.

"Woof!" Dylan jumped free of Megan's grasp, ran in a mad circle, then followed Buster and Lauren.

"Time for the Mystery Pups to spring into action!" Lauren cried. "Come on, let's go!"

CHAPTER THREE

In the street there was chaos. Cops stopped the traffic. Cab drivers got out of their cars and started to yell impatiently. Meanwhile, a dozen police officers ran up the steps into the tallest, flashiest building on the avenue.

It was Buster who first dashed between a bystander's legs and made a run towards the entrance.

"Mercury Movies." Lauren read the sign above the door. *Cool!* she thought, dashing after her pup. *Maybe a mega-famous film star has gone missing!*

Megan and Caitlin weren't far behind.

They read the name and peered into the swish entrance lobby. The floor was white marble. The reception desk was made of glass and steel.

"Maybe someone got shot!" Caitlin gasped.

"Let's hope not." Megan watched Dylan and Daisy weave between the legs of cops and office workers. No one paid them any attention as they scampered across the crowded lobby.

"Stand back!" a police officer ordered the gathering crowd. "We need to keep the entrance clear!"

Two men began to section off the entrance to the building with orange tape. "No one leaves the building," the cops ordered. "Not until we've checked you out."

Caitlin and Megan caught up with Lauren. They managed to grab their pups and fade into the background as people piled out of the elevators, shouting and protesting. "What's happened? Did someone die? Why are we locked in?"

"OK!" Megan said, drawing a long breath. "As usual, Dylan, Buster and Daisy have landed us in the middle of something massive!"

"Yeah, so much for snoozing in the park," Lauren agreed.

"What happens when the police question us?" Caitlin asked.

"We play dumb," Lauren decided. "We say we don't even know what all the fuss is about."

"Which we don't," Megan pointed out. "All we know is that we're inside a building where they make movies. I suppose there are studios and stuff here where they shoot the films."

"And there'll be actors!" Caitlin said excitedly. "Matt Pitman, Kali Knight, Jake Wood…!" She listed her favourite stars.

"And a heap of angry people all wanting to know what's going on," Lauren added. "But, listen – if we say we haven't a clue what's happening, the police will let us go, which is not what we want."

"It isn't?" a puzzled Caitlin asked.

"No, we want to stay here and do our sleuthing – you know; let the pups sniff around and discover clues, like they usually do. We can't do that if the police tell us to leave."

"So we keep quiet and stay in the background," Megan agreed. "We try to sneak off further into the building when no one's looking."

"Yap!" Buster let out a loud bark.

"Sshh! That's just what we *don't* need," Lauren groaned.

Luckily, at that moment the lift doors opened and one of the brightest stars in the movie firmament walked out. He was tall and broad-shouldered, his dark hair flecked with grey and he was dressed in a checked shirt, jeans and cowboy boots.

'It's Jake Wood!" Caitlin swooned as the superstar walked close by. "My mum loves him!"

The actor was surrounded by assistants. They cleared the way towards the exit so that Jake could walk easily through the crowd.

"Sorry, sir!" The cop guarding the door pointed to the orange tape. "No one leaves the building."

Jake frowned then put on his most charming smile. "Hey, it's me," he said to the police officer. "You know who I am, don't you?"

"Yes sir, Mr Wood," the officer said. "But those are my orders."

The big star shrugged. "OK, I hear you," he muttered, stepping back.

"I can't believe it's him – Jake Wood – in the flesh!" Caitlin whispered.

"A total superstar!" Megan sighed. "I read in a gossip mag that he's making a film about Billy the Kid."

Just then a blonde woman in a black suit stepped out of the lift.

Loud cries flew around the lobby. "Thelma Taylor!... The boss! Quiet, everyone... Miss Taylor's here... Let's listen to what she has to say!"

Caitlin, Megan and Lauren watched the woman walk over to the shiny reception desk. She got ready to read from a piece of paper.

"Hey, everyone, we're sorry about all this," she began in a loud, clear voice. "I've spoken with the police officer in charge here and he's cleared me to make a statement."

"Seems like you need a permit to breathe around here!" Jake Wood joked, loud enough for everyone to hear.

Thelma Taylor didn't smile. "Something very serious has occurred, which is why we've closed the building. You'll all be aware that Mercury Movies has just begun filming the sequel to our runaway hit, *Candy, Come Home*. Shooting began early this morning."

"*Candy*. . . Wasn't that the blockbuster about the cat that got lost and walked hundreds of miles to find her owners?" Megan whispered.

Lauren and Caitlin nodded. "It was amazing!" Caitlin hissed.

Thelma Taylor hushed the murmurs. "You'll be aware also of how much this sequel means to Mercury. It's our major project this year. And it all depends on the safety and well-being of Jasmine, its very special feline star."

"Don't tell me – the cat croaked!" One of Jake Wood's companions risked another joke.

There was a shocked silence.

"This is serious," Miss Taylor said sternly. "Jasmine, otherwise known as Candy, arrived at the studio with her trainer early this morning. Ryan Cooper, the director, filmed a couple of short scenes that didn't require Jasmine. When he eventually called for her, they couldn't find either the trainer or Jasmine herself, though there were signs of a struggle in the corridor. We called the police in right away. It seems the star of our movie has been snatched from right under our noses!"

CHAPTER FOUR

"You're telling me we're all stuck here because of a *cat*?" As usual, Jake Wood didn't mince words.

After Thelma Taylor's speech, the police had carried on bringing everyone in the building down to the ground floor. Now the lift doors stood open and more than a hundred employees stood in line waiting to be interviewed.

Caitlin, Megan and Lauren kept in a huddle behind the large glass desk. Their pups crouched at their sides.

"Poor little kitty!" Caitlin whispered. "Mum

loves cats so she took me to see the film – it was amazing how they got the cat to do stuff like balancing on a tree branch to cross a river. Cats don't like water, but Jasmine's been specially trained."

"What does she look like?" Megan asked.

"She's pretty unusual – pale grey with big green eyes – *so* cute!"

"So she's no ordinary moggy?" Lauren said.

"No way!" Caitlin insisted. "Like I said, she's trained to do what the director wants – she's really clever!"

"Which makes her very special," Megan said thoughtfully. "And very valuable."

"So you think she's been kidnapped?" Lauren asked.

"Cat-napped!" Megan nodded.

At her feet, Dylan gave a yap, as if agreeing. He stood up and wagged his tail.

"Yes, I know, Dylan – you think we should be searching the building," Megan murmured.

"Me too!" Lauren agreed. "Listen – you see that stairway at the back of the lobby?"

Megan and Caitlin nodded.

"Do you think we can get over there without anyone noticing?"

"Difficult," Megan warned. "And we don't want to attract attention to ourselves."

"But if we don't sneak up the stairs, we'll just get questioned and sent on our way," Caitlin figured. "I'm with Lauren. I think we should risk it. Send the pups ahead."

"You hear that?" Lauren said to Buster, Dylan and Daisy. "Make your way to the stairs without a sound!"

As it happened, Jake Wood himself was currently being quizzed by the cops.

"No, I don't know where the cat is!" he told them with his charming smile. "Do I *look* like a guy who would steal a cat?"

Everyone's attention was fixed on the superstar, so the girls seized their chance.

Sending the pups ahead, Lauren, Caitlin, then Megan, crept silently towards the shadowy stairway at the back of the lobby.

"Made it!" Megan breathed a sigh of relief as she and Dylan leaped up the stairs two at a time.

Buster and Daisy were already on the first landing, sniffing at the doors that led off down different corridors.

"No, not that way!" Lauren decided as she caught sight of police activity. "Let's go up another storey."

And so they went up and up, spotting cops at every level, until they came to the thirtieth floor.

"It looks like the police began their search at the bottom of the building and are working their way up," Caitlin said, out of breath after the long climb.

"So we start here, at the top, and work our way down," Lauren decided.

Buster, Dylan and Daisy seemed to agree. They ran to a door marked Studio 5 and scratched for it to be opened. "Yip! Yap!" they barked.

"Hush!" Megan warned, pushing open the door and discovering a huge room with bright lights, cameras and sound equipment all focused on a small set representing an old-fashioned saloon bar, with glasses and a row of bottles on a shelf behind. There was a clapperboard thrown carelessly onto the bar top saying, "Billy the Kid, Scene 36."

"This is where Jake Wood was filming!" Caitlin said, while the pups poked their noses into every corner of the studio. Once they'd checked everywhere, they came back to the girls.

"No sign of Jasmine?" Megan asked.

"Woof!" Dylan seemed to say that they needed to move on.

"Let's see what's further down the corridor," Lauren suggested, leading the way with Buster.

"An empty office," she said, glancing to her left. Then she went on. "Another office."

"What's in here?" Caitlin opened the door into a small, dark store room. There were brushes and brooms leaning against the wall, and a grey locker in one corner.

Daisy took a sniff around the room then yapped. She raced straight up to the tall metal locker.

"Hey, Daisy might be on to something!" Caitlin called the others.

"Woof! Yap!" Buster and Dylan ran to join Daisy, jumping up at the locker door and scratching at the handle.

"It's locked!"

Caitlin pulled hard at the door.

From inside the locker she heard a muffled cry.

"Somebody's trapped," Megan muttered. "Come here, Lauren. Let's all pull together – maybe we can force the lock!"

So the three girls pulled with all their strength until the thin metal door buckled and the lock gave way. They stepped back quickly as a girl rolled out of the locker onto the store room floor.

CHAPTER FIVE

The girl's hands were tied behind her back and she was gagged.

"Quick, we have to untie her!" Megan stooped and began to loosen the gag.

Lauren and Caitlin worked on the knots that bound her hands and feet.

"Where's Jasmine?" the girl gasped as soon as she could speak. She was about thirteen, with short black hair, wearing jeans and a loose white top. "Did they stop the guy who snatched her? Tell me they caught him - please!"

"Calm down," Caitlin said, as she and Lauren helped the gasping girl to her feet.

"Are you Jasmine's trainer?" Megan asked.

The girl nodded. "I'm Gemma Stone, Caroline Stone's daughter. Mom runs Animal Allstars – an agency for animals who appear in movies. She told me to guard Jasmine with my life!"

"But you say someone snatched her?" Lauren asked. "And the same guy tied you up and stuck you in that locker?"

Gemma nodded. "He jumped me from behind. I'm not very big, and he was strong. He was wearing sunglasses and a cap, so I didn't get a good look at his face."

"Where were you when this happened?" Megan asked.

"In the office next door. I was waiting there with Jasmine until Ryan Cooper needed us down in Studio 3."

"OK, Buster, you three go and take a look next door." Megan opened the store room door to let the pups out into the corridor.

"Are you OK?" Caitlin checked with Gemma. "The man didn't hurt you?"

"No. But I was scared to death. Everything happened so quickly I couldn't even yell for help."

"And are you sure he took Jasmine?"

"I'm not sure about anything! After he locked me in there I don't know *what* happened."

Just then, Dylan reappeared. Between his teeth he carried a pair of expensive sports sunglasses. Not far behind, Daisy and Buster showed up. Buster was carrying a dark blue baseball cap.

"Good dogs!" Megan took the items from them. "Now go and look again. Go find!"

The Labrador pup, the little mongrel and the Yorkie trotted off obediently.

"Are those the glasses and the cap the man was wearing?" Caitlin asked Gemma, who by now had caught her breath.

She nodded. "Mom will kill me if anything happens to Jasmine. I had to beg her to let me bring her in today – it's the school vacation, so I have time on my hands, and I love watching them make the movie."

"You'd better talk to the police," Lauren decided, as Caitlin went to find the pups.

Dylan, Buster and Daisy were busy picking up scents in the corridor, gathering near a door marked Fire Escape, yipping and yapping to attract her attention. "They've found a trail!" Caitlin called to Lauren and Megan.

Megan took a quick decision. "OK, Gemma. All you have to do is go down a couple of floors in the lift – you'll find cops everywhere. Show them the sunglasses and the cap, and tell them the whole story, OK?"

Gemma nodded. "What about you?"

"We'll follow the puppies," Megan explained. "There's no time to explain, but they're kind of special – let's just say they know what they're doing!"

With this, Megan and Lauren ran to join Caitlin and the pups.

"Help me to push this metal bar," Caitlin muttered. "It's stiff."

Pushing together, the girls managed to open the Fire Escape door and the puppies bounded on to a metal staircase that went all the way down to ground level.

"I bet this was the cat-napper's getaway route," Caitlin decided. "Look, Daisy's leading the way!"

Down thirty floors the puppies went, their feet pattering on the metal stairs, with Caitlin, Lauren and Megan following close behind. Through the windows of the tower block, the girls saw corridors with police on guard. Once, they thought a cop had spotted them so they picked up speed and reached the ground before he could open the window to investigate.

"Duck down!" Lauren gasped. She made them all hide behind some giant wheelie bins until the coast was clear.

The policeman came out onto the metal landing and peered over the rail. He saw nothing, shook his head and went back inside.

"We made it," Megan murmured, giving Dylan a quick hug. "Now it's over to you, Daisy and Buster again!"

Outside on the main street, traffic was slowly getting back to normal, though the police cordon around the Mercury Movies building was still in place.

Mixing with the crowd, Buster, Daisy and Dylan tried hard to pick up the cat thief's trail.

"This will cost Mercury millions!" a woman in the crowd was saying.

"Yeah, not one single scene in that movie will get made until they get Jasmine back," her neighbour agreed.

"Hey look, here comes Jake Wood!" someone else cried as the mega-star strode down the steps and a thousand cameras clicked.

"Hi everyone, it's not every day I get upstaged by a cat!" he grinned.

The actor's minders shoved their way to the edge of the pavement.

"Look this way, Jake! Give me an autograph! Hey, let my friend take a picture of me with you!"

Jake posed for pictures, then climbed into the back of a silver limousine and told the driver to step on the gas. The car screeched away from the kerb.

It was a signal for the crowd to melt away. They'd had a glimpse of a major star – they'd got a blurred picture and a story to tell when they got home. Soon the way was clear for the girls and their pups to cross the wide road and go back into the park.

CHAPTER SIX

"This feels like a dead end," Lauren sighed.

Buster, Dylan and Daisy sniffed along the joggers' path, zig-zagging this way and that. They seemed to have lost the cat thief's trail.

"Maybe we should have stayed inside the building and found more clues," Caitlin said.

"No," Megan argued. "It was the pups who wanted us to leave by the Fire Escape, remember. And like I told Gemma, they're very smart!"

"Anyway, we did learn some important stuff," Lauren realised, following Buster towards the lake. "We know the thief wore a disguise –

the glasses and the cap - while he was inside Mercury, but not when he came out."

The girls were silent for a while, watching Buster, Dylan and Daisy work at picking up the scent. The pups went along the lakeside, noses to the ground, little tails wagging.

"It's not much to go on, is it?" Caitlin admitted after a while. "I mean, we've no idea who would want to kidnap poor Jasmine, or why."

"It could be someone who's jealous of her success," Megan said thoughtfully.

"Or someone who wanted to stop this sequel being made."

"A rival film-maker!" Lauren nodded. "That's it, Megan! We need to know - who else makes movies with animals as heroes?"

"Whoa-whoa!" Caitlin raised both hands. "Hold on a second. Lauren, hadn't you'd better go and rescue Buster?"

"Uh-oh!" Lauren groaned and ran to drag her puppy away from the old woman who'd

been reading a book when they first arrived in the park. Buster was jumping up and yapping, tugging at the woman's skirt. She was trying to bat him away with her novel.

"Sorry!" Lauren said breathlessly. "He's not usually like this!"

"They all say that," the old woman grumbled. "Every owner thinks their dog is well-trained, even when they're chewing a stranger's skirt or yapping at her feet!"

"Down, Buster!" Lauren pleaded, as her

boisterous pet jumped up and barked. "Don't take this the wrong way," she gabbled to the woman. "But do you think Buster is picking up a scent?"

Megan and Caitlin caught up with Lauren to hear the woman's reply.

"What do you mean, picking up a scent?" she demanded, finally closing her book and standing up.

"Sorry – Lauren didn't mean to be rude," Caitlin stepped in. "It's just that our puppies are picking up an important trail – you heard about Jasmine going missing, didn't you?"

"Jasmine who?" The woman ran a hand through her wild, curly hair. "I don't know anyone called Jasmine."

"Jasmine is a cat superstar," Caitlin explained. She struggled to keep Daisy from jumping up at the woman. "She starred in *Candy, Come Home* – the story about the cat who walked miles and miles to find her owners after she got lost in the mountains. Mercury

Movies have just started filming *Candy 2*."

The woman stared back. "What in the world are you talking about? Listen, I never go to that kind of kid movie. Now would you please put your dogs on a leash and go away!"

"Sorry, we don't know why they're behaving like this," Megan told her. Even Dylan had begun to pester the stranger. "They only bother people if they're following up a clue…" Suddenly Megan stopped. It sounded mad, but she began to wonder if this old lady with her head stuck deep in a book actually *could* help them track down the missing feline superstar. "You've been here a long time, haven't you?" she asked.

"Since early this morning," the woman said sniffily. "I come here every day, I sit on this bench and keep to my own personal space."

"But you see people come and go?" Megan asked more hopefully, pleased to see that Buster, Daisy and Dylan had calmed down at last.

They sat on the grass while the woman gave her grudging, grumpy answers.

"Nothing gets by me," Book-lady told the girls.

"I like to people-watch. It's a hobby of mine, if you must know."

"So did you see anyone unusual today?" Megan prompted, trying to be super-polite.

"No. Today has been normal. Except for this stupid fuss with the police cars on the Avenue. I wondered what it was about. And now you tell me it's all to do with a famous cat going missing?"

Megan nodded eagerly. "A beautiful grey cat."

"With green eyes." Caitlin completed the description.

"Hmmm." The woman narrowed her eyes thoughtfully. "That figures."

"It does?" Lauren's eyes lit up. "So you did see something after all? We're searching for a man with a cat. What we want to know is – did he make his getaway across the park?"

"Let me begin at the beginning," the book-lady said, sitting down on her bench. She made Lauren, Caitlin and Megan sit down on the grass next to their puppies.

"Like I said, I was here early – hoping for a quiet read – when a young guy stopped by this bench."

The girls nodded eagerly.

"He was dressed like all the other joggers around here," the woman went on. "Jogging pants and trainers. He was carrying a rucksack, and when he stopped, he took out a pair of sunglasses and a cap, and he put them on."

"What colour was the bag?" Megan asked.

"Blue," the woman declared.

"Go on!" Lauren said, almost too excited to breathe.

"Well, there was nothing too unusual about that. After he put on the cap and glasses, he put the rucksack back on his back. Then he went on his way. That's it."

"What did he look like?" Lauren quizzed. "Was he tall? What colour was his hair?"

"I'd say he was a good-looking young guy – fair-haired, handsome enough to be in movies himself, like a lot of the kids you see round here. They hang around the doors of the

Mercury building, hoping to be talent-spotted, I guess."

"And was that it?" Caitlin asked. "Did anything else happen after that?"

"Hold it a second. Let me catch my breath," the woman replied, reminding them of a strict school teacher. "Something else *did* happen – not too long after I first saw you and your puppies. I was deep into my book again and the same young guy came back into the park. He broke into my personal space, and I didn't like it."

"Why? What did he do?" Lauren asked.

"He was running fast – sprinting. But he stopped at this bench again and slid the rucksack off his back to take a quick look inside. He seemed hot and harassed. And of course, this all begins to make sense now."

"What does?" Lauren, Caitlin and Megan chorused.

"This young guy in a hurry took time to unzip the bag and peek into it. And just as he opened it, I thought I heard him speak."

"Was he talking to someone on his phone?" Megan asked.

The old lady shook her head. "No, he was either talking to himself or to something hidden in the rucksack. And now it looks like it was the latter."

"Oh!" Caitlin gasped.

Jasmine's fate was clear to her, Megan and Lauren now. The jogger had gone into the Mercury building, snatched the poor cat, stuffed her inside a dark rucksack and fled through the park.

CHAPTER SEVEN

"We saw the kidnapper!" Megan insisted after the sharp-eyed lady had finished her story. "The cat thief actually sprinted towards us - remember?"

Megan nodded. "We were *this* close!" she reminded Lauren and Caitlin

"If only we'd known!" Lauren groaned. "We could have stopped him in his tracks and Jasmine would be safe!"

"Hush. Let's think this through." There was no time for regrets - Megan tried to concentrate on what the old lady had told them. "Did you notice anything else?"

"As a matter of fact I did." Still unmoved by the drama surrounding her, she slid an envelope from inside the cover of her book. "This letter fell from his bag and in his hurry he left it behind. I decided to post it for him. It's addressed to Thelma Taylor."

"Woof!" At last! Dylan, Daisy and Buster edged closer. Quick as a flash, Buster jumped up and snatched the letter from the old lady's hand. Then he darted off across the park towards the exit onto the broad Avenue.

"Hey!" the book-lady cried.

"Sorry! But don't worry – we'll make sure the letter gets delivered," Caitlin assured her. Lauren, Megan, Daisy and Dylan had already set off after Buster and she was eager to follow. "And thank you – you've helped us so much! Bye!"

The girls and the pups raced back through the park once more – past the mothers with their prams and the endless flow of joggers, past the lake with the nervous ducks, to the wide gates onto the Avenue.

They only stopped at the kerb for the crossing lights to change to green then they rushed over the road, under the orange police cordon and up the shiny steps of the Mercury building.

"Stop! You can't go in!" A burly cop guarded the door. He stuck out his foot to trip Buster, but the clever pup swerved and darted between his legs.

"Nobody enters the building!" the cop repeated, standing in the path of Dylan, Daisy and the girls.

"Sorry, it's my pup, Buster – he got away from me," Lauren fibbed. "I'm trying to train him, but he's a real handful!"

"Huh!" the police officer glanced over his

shoulder to see the madcap but harmless mongrel zooming across the marble floor. "I guess you'd better go in and fetch him. But make it snappy."

"Wait here!" Lauren hissed to the others. Then she disappeared into the building.

She found that the lobby was almost empty now, except for a few police officers and Thelma Taylor herself.

"This is a tough problem, Ryan," the boss of Mercury was saying to her companion –

a small, balding man with a shaven head and a silver earring.

"What we know, according to Gemma Stone, is that a single guy carried out the kidnapping, without any accomplices. The police have interviewed her and got all the information they could, but we're nowhere nearer to finding out who the guy is or where he's taken the cat."

"I'm devastated," Ryan Cooper confessed. "This totally wrecks my filming schedule!"

"Here, Buster!" Lauren chased her pup across the shiny floor. She wanted to seize her chance and hand the letter over to Thelma Taylor in person.

Buster did one more circuit of the lobby then stopped dead beside Miss Taylor.

The big boss glanced down at the scruffy pup with an envelope in its mouth. "Who let this mutt in to the building?" she frowned.

"The letter's for you!" Lauren gasped, without

stopping to explain. "It's from the cat-napper!"

"Back off, kid." Ryan Cooper stepped forward and tried to shoo Buster towards the entrance. "Don't bother us, OK?"

"No, wait." Thelma Taylor had seen her own name written on the envelope. She looked warily at Buster. "Will he bite?" she asked.

"Here, Buster, give the letter to me," Lauren ordered, taking it and handing it over to Thelma, who ripped it open.

"'Two million, or you never see the cat again!'" Thelma read out the simple message. "Two *million*? That's quite some ransom!"

"I knew it would cost us a fortune to get Jasmine back," Cooper groaned. Then he shot a suspicious look at Lauren. "How come *you* had this letter?"

"It's a long story," she replied. Her heart was beating fast as she wondered what Thelma Taylor would do next.

Carefully and calmly Miss Taylor folded the note and slid it back into its envelope. "No way will we pay!" she said in a clear, determined voice.

Lauren's heart thudded, then missed a beat. "But what about Jasmine?" she stammered. "What'll happen to her if you don't pay the ransom?"

Thelma Taylor shrugged. "No cat is worth two million," she said coldly.

"What's going on? Is this kid bothering you?" a cop asked, laying his hand on Lauren's arm.

Shaking her head as if swatting away a fly, the boss of Mercury turned towards her director. "Don't worry, Ryan. This picture will still get made, and it won't cost us an extra cent, trust me!"

CHAPTER EIGHT

"The movie will still get made!" Caitlin exclaimed.

She sat with Lauren, Megan and the pups on the train to the outskirts of Sleuth City. Grids of streets lined with tall buildings and crawling with traffic spread to either side as far as the eye could see.

"How can Ryan Cooper go on filming the *Candy* sequel without its major star?"

"I have no idea," Lauren answered. Inside the Mercury building she'd been through a strict grilling by the police – "So, kid, where did you get this ransom note? What do you know about the guy who wrote it? Come on, tell us!"

After the police had let Lauren go, she'd reported back to Megan and Caitlin and the girls had decided that they should talk to Gemma Stone again.

It had mostly been Megan's idea. "We have to find out more about how they work with animal actors. And we need to tell Gemma that Thelma Taylor has turned down the ransom demand."

Caitlin had remembered the name, Animal Allstars, and they'd searched for an address in the internet café in the park. They'd come up with a street on the edge of town.

So the train rattled through the city and Dylan, Daisy and Buster took a well-earned rest at the girls' feet.

"Thelma Taylor is a scary lady," Lauren told Caitlin and Megan. "Cold as a block of ice. I don't think she cares about Jasmine one little bit."

"But *we* do!" Caitlin insisted. "And Gemma

does, too. You could tell she was upset about what had happened."

"So let's go and talk to her." Lauren stood up as they reached the station they wanted. She led the way onto the platform and out to the street. "Can you tell us the way to Animal Allstars on Hill Street?" she asked the first person who passed by.

Soon the girls and the pups arrived at an ordinary, glass-fronted building with a small name plate which told them they'd come to the right place. Megan rang the bell.

They waited a long time but at last a woman came to the door. "Yes?" she said sharply.

Megan looked in at a large room lined with pet cages – clean and hygienic like a vet's reception room, with a smooth, grey floor and strip lights on the ceiling.

"We've come to see Gemma," Lauren said, boldly stepping forward. She took in the smartly-dressed, middle-aged woman with carefully styled, dyed blonde hair and glossy pink fingernails. "Are you her mother?"

"Who's asking?" the woman asked, darting suspicious looks from the girls to the pups. "We don't need any more animals on our books," she warned. "Our lists are full right now."

"It's OK, Mom," a tired voice said from inside the room. Then Gemma came to the door. "I've already met them. They're the kids who found me in the locker and untied me. Can they come in?"

"Meet Bandit. He's a red-heeled lurcher," Gemma said, opening a cage door and letting Caitlin see a grey-and-brown speckled hunting dog about five times the size of Daisy. The fearless Yorkie wagged her tail in greeting.

"Bandit starred in a road movie called *Route 66*," Gemma said, giving the dog a friendly stroke.

"Hello, Bandit – you're famous!" Caitlin cried. "Wow, you're sweet too!"

From along the row of cages, other dogs barked and cats miaowed.

"First, we've got some bad news." Megan took on the job of talking to the owner of Animal Allstars – a woman who was better groomed and manicured than the showiest show dog in town, she decided. "Lauren was in the building when Thelma Taylor turned down the ransom demand for Jasmine. She says no way is Mercury going to pay!"

"She was really cruel about it," Lauren added. "We're very sorry."

"Tell me some news that really *is* new," Caroline Stone said in a flat voice. "Listen, kid – I already got the phone call from Thelma's assistant. It's true – they have a business to run. If they can find a solution without losing two million, well – it makes sense to me."

Lauren and Megan stood open-mouthed at this reply, while Caitlin saw Gemma choke back her own feelings.

Lauren was the first to speak. "I don't believe you just said that! Don't you care what happens to Jasmine?"

"Yes, of course I care. But I'm a business person too," Caroline argued. "In this line of work you can't afford to be sentimental."

In the background, the animals barked and miaowed from their cages.

"But we're talking about a real live animal here," Megan protested. "Besides, she's a movie superstar. We thought you'd be desperate to get Jasmine back!"

"Hey, drop it, will you?" Gemma begged, her eyes full of tears.

The girls seemed to have irritated the Allstars boss. "Sure, Jasmine is a big star," she admitted. "But this kidnapper is as naive as you three kids if he thinks that Jasmine is the only cat who can play this role in *Candy 2*!"

Caitlin stared in disbelief at Gemma. "What is she talking about?"

"Come here." Reluctantly Caroline's daughter gestured the girls towards three luxury cat cages lined up on a wide shelf.

She opened the doors one at a time and handed first Caitlin, then Lauren, and finally Megan, the cats who were snuggled up inside.

Three grey cats with soft, smooth coats. Three cats with green eyes. Just like Jasmine.

"Meet Cleo, Wilma and Sugar," Gemma said quietly. "When you're filming a movie with animals you always have to make sure you have at least four identikit versions!"

"It's all my fault," Gemma told Caitlin, Lauren and Megan.

They were back on the train with the pups, not knowing what else to do except go back to the park where it had all begun.

Gemma had argued with her mother and slammed the door on Animal Allstars. "OK, Mom, I hear you! You don't care about Jasmine, but *I* do. I'm going to help these girls find her!"

"I blame myself for not taking better care of Jasmine," she confessed as they got off the train and headed for the park. "None of this would have happened if it hadn't been for me."

"No way!" Caitlin protested. "Listen, you're

the only one who even cares what happens to Jasmine. And look – Daisy, Dylan and Buster like you!"

Tails up once more, the three pups trotted beside Gemma, leading her through the park gates.

"And you've shown us what a mean trick the film makers play on the audience," Megan added. "They should tell us that Candy is four different cats – otherwise it's a big con!"

"But that would spoil everything," Gemma explained. "They need stand-ins, just in case one of the cats isn't well, or if one won't do a certain thing that the director wants her to do."

"We still think it's a mean trick," Caitlin insisted.

"But in one way, your mother was right," Megan pointed out. "The kidnapper didn't realise that Thelma Taylor would easily find a way around the problem of the ransom. Which means he or she didn't know much about animal actors and how it all works."

"So who could it be?" Lauren sighed, looking around the peaceful park. She felt helpless as she watched the picnickers and the strollers, the joggers and the folk feeding the ducks. "It's like looking for a needle in a haystack, isn't it, Buster?"

Her scruffy pup sat on the grass and looked up at her with bright eyes. "Yip!" he said. *Don't give in. Together we can do this!* "Yap! Yap!"

CHAPTER NINE

It was at moments like this that Lauren, Megan and Caitlin knew they had to trust their mystery pups.

Don't give in! Buster seemed to say, while Dylan put his nose to the ground and made a beeline for the café. Daisy yipped at Gemma and told her to follow.

"The café it is!" Megan hurried after Dylan.

The little black Labrador was already mingling with customers at the outside tables, busily sniffing and investigating. Soon Buster and Daisy joined him.

A young waitress came out of the café and

spied the pups. "Cute!" she beamed, then straight away went to fill a plastic dish with water. She put the dish on the ground near to the entrance.

Buster, Dylan and Daisy slurped noisily, tails in the air. The four girls sat at a table nearby.

"I don't know what to think," Gemma sighed. "To me, it looks like some random guy from the street decided it was a good idea to kidnap Jasmine and demand a ransom, and in that case it's going to be really hard to trace him."

"But how did he get into the Mercury building?" Megan asked. "He needed a pass, like the one you're wearing."

Gemma glanced down at the plastic label still pinned to her shirt. It showed her picture beside a printed name and number.

"Which means it's an inside job!" Lauren said, suddenly excited. "Hey, I never thought of that before."

"Probably," Megan admitted. "But don't let's jump to conclusions."

"Who do you know with a grudge against Jasmine or someone else in the movie?" Caitlin pressed Gemma for an answer.

"I can tell you that, no problem!" The waitress, who had been busy wiping tables, broke in with the latest gossip. She was small and slim, with fair hair lifted into a spiky ponytail. "We just had Jake Wood here in the café."

"So?" Lauren frowned.

"Yip!" Buster jumped up onto Lauren's knee, ears pricked, listening to the waitress's explanation.

"He snuck in here to escape his fans on his way back to work. Everyone wants a piece of the gorgeous Jake Wood. I see a lot of movie stars in here and he's one I really don't like – he loves himself way too much."

Megan narrowed her eyes. "Are you saying he has some kind of grudge against Jasmine?"

The waitress nodded. "So would you, if you were a huge star and your movie had charted second to a kids' film about a cat. Think about it – movie goers are starting to prefer cute little Candy to hunky Jake Wood!"

"Is that true?" Caitlin asked Gemma doubtfully.

Gemma nodded. "Jake Wood's ratings are definitely on the slide. People say this Billy the Kid role is his last chance before the movie backers ditch him."

"So anyway," the waitress went on. "Jake Wood dashes in here with a wannabe actor –

a young guy named Zak Greenberg. My manager agrees to sneak them out the back way. But I overhear Zak and Jake talking and Jake is enjoying the fact that the *Candy* movie is on hold because the cat has vanished."

"What did he say exactly?" Lauren asked.

"Word for word, Jake says, 'Now my movie will be the top Mercury movie of the year!'" the waitress recalled. "And he was grinning when he said it, and laughing with his dumb sidekick."

"Wow!" Caitlin gasped. Who'd have suspected it of the A-list star?

"What did Zak look like?" Megan tried to keep calm. This was brilliant stuff from the chilled, chatty waitress.

The girl shrugged. "He looked like the usual bit-part

actor – tall, fair hair, tanned. I didn't pay too much attention."

Lauren jumped to her feet. "What was he wearing?"

"Let me see. Yeah – jogging pants and running shoes."

"Yes!" Lauren punched the air. She beamed at the puzzled waitress. "That's so cool! You've been amazing. Thank you!"

"Ready?" Gemma asked.

She stood with Lauren, Caitlin and Megan at the entrance to the Mercury building. The pups stayed obediently to heel.

The girls nodded and held their breaths. It was a risky plan that they'd decided on as they'd dashed through the park, but they knew that if they wanted to save Jasmine before she came to harm they had to act fast.

"OK, let's go!" Swinging through the doors, Gemma led the way to the reception desk.

The girl on duty glanced at the procession of children and puppies marching across the marble floor. "Yes?" she said crossly.

Gemma showed her pass. "My mom's the boss of Animal Allstars," she told the receptionist. "We're due in Studio 3."

"*All* of you?" the woman asked doubtfully.

Daisy, Buster and Dylan held their heads high, trying their best to look like the pedigree pampered pets on the Allstars list.

Gemma nodded and stuck to the prearranged story. "These puppies are booked in for a crowd scene in the *Candy* movie. The girls too. We got an urgent phone call from the director, Ryan Cooper. He's had to reschedule because of the kidnapping."

"No need to tell me," the receptionist heaved a tired sigh and let them through. "What a day we've had here!"

"Thanks!" Gemma led the way to the lift before the receptionist could change her mind. "Good work, everyone - we're in!" she hissed.

Lights flashed on the wall panel and the lift arrived. The girls and the pups stepped in.

"Forget Studio 3. We're going straight up to Level 30 to find Jake Wood," Gemma muttered, pressing the buttons again.

"We're going to nail him, the lousy cheat!" Lauren vowed as the lift glided upwards.

"And Zak the cat-napper!" Caitlin added.

"Before it's too late," Megan whispered, afraid

for poor Jasmine who was caught in the middle of this mess.

They fell silent and crossed their fingers, waiting for the lift to stop.

At last the doors opened onto a corridor, empty except for two figures arguing in the distance.

"That's them!" Caitlin gasped, recognising the dark-haired actor and his blond friend.

But as soon as the two men realised they'd been spotted, they broke apart and set off in different directions. Meanwhile, Thelma Taylor herself turned a corner and came stalking down the corridor.

"Oh, Jake!" she called in a loud, confident voice.

The actor squared his shoulders and strutted towards her. "Hey Thelma," he drawled. "Sorry to hear about the problems on the *Candy* set. But I guess it's just one of those things."

Thelma narrowed her eyes. "The news about Jasmine leaked out right away," she admitted. "The press got onto it. This kidnap is going to be headline news – plus the fact that I'm refusing to pay the ransom."

"Yeah?" Jake found it hard not to give away his reaction. Shock registered on his face before he found his usual joking tone. "So it really *is* bad news for the cat. And the entire movie bites the dust. But luckily, you still have me to head up the new releases this year."

"You mean, lucky for you, huh, Jake?" Thelma seemed about to walk on, but then she turned. "By the way, it seems you didn't you hear the latest piece of good news – we can carry on shooting the *Candy* movie exactly as planned."

Jake took a step backwards. He seemed confused.

Thelma smiled coldly at him. "The fact is, the kidnapper was too dumb to realise we have three stand-in cats who can also play the role."

The movie star shook his head. He tried to laugh but it came out as a croak.

"Stupid, huh?" Thelma said, turning away again and striding off down the corridor towards the bunch of girls and puppies.

"You're on the wrong floor," she told them, arching her eyebrows as Dylan, Daisy and Buster surrounded her. "You need Level 25, Studio 3 for *Candy 2*. Now, shoo, pups, shoo!"

CHAPTER TEN

Caitlin, Megan, Lauren and Gemma waited until Thelma had disappeared into the lift.

"Did you *see* Jake's face when he found out his plan hadn't worked?" Lauren cried.

"He's guilty all right. But we still have to get him to admit what he did and tell us where Jasmine is now," Megan reminded them. "And that's not going to be easy."

"Let's split up," Caitlin decided. "Lauren and Megan, you take Buster and Dylan. Spy on Jake Wood – watch his every move. Sooner or later he's bound to give himself away!"

"What will you, Daisy and Gemma do?" Megan asked.

"We'll find Zak Greenberg and do the same," Caitlin replied. "If any of us get into trouble, send one of the pups to find the others, OK?"

"Good plan," Megan agreed. "Let's go!"

"Where's Jake? Has anybody seen him?" The director of *Billy the Kid* – an old man with a shock of white hair – stalked the studio floor. He looked at his watch, then muttered under his breath.

Megan and Lauren had crept in through a side door. They hid with Dylan and Buster behind a large camera on a metal stand. Wires trailed across the floor and the studio lights were dim.

"Jake's still in make-up,"

an assistant said, trying to keep the director calm.

It was the signal for the two pups to sneak out again, closely followed by Megan and Lauren, who raced down the corridor, into the lift and up to Level 30, where they tracked down the actor in the cluttered make-up room.

"Wait!" Megan hissed at Dylan and Buster as they reached the open door.

"Zak Greenberg was heading towards the back stairs when we last saw him," Caitlin reminded Gemma.

Daisy beat them to it. Nose to the ground, the tiny pup headed straight for the stairs and down to the basement. From there she ran across a big car park and through the underground entrance of Sleuth City Central Fitness Club.

"You see that?" Caitlin pointed out the sign over the entrance. "Daisy's definitely on to something. Good girl – you're doing a brilliant job!"

"Sshh!" Gemma warned, following the puppy to the door of the men's changing-room.

"What do I do now?" a man's voice said from inside. "I lost the ransom note and totally screwed up. Now I'll never get the movie role Jake promised me for doing this – that's the only reason I agreed!"

"That sounds like Zak!" Gemma hissed in the silence that followed. "He's speaking on the phone. Listen!"

"Suddenly it's all gone wrong," Zak went on. "Jake's totally lost it – I mean, big time! You know how he is. He won't even speak to me."

"Stand back!" Caitlin warned the others as Zak's voice grew louder.

He came out into the corridor. She, Gemma and Daisy tried to act naturally.

"OK, I'm definitely going to talk to Jake before he goes on set," Zak said into his phone. He ignored Caitlin and the others. "Yeah, I

know – this is too important – I'll sprint back over to the studio and do it now."

"They can wait until I'm ready!" high and mighty Jake told the make-up girl. "Nobody pushes Jake Wood around!"

Lauren and Megan grimaced as they listened from outside the door. The movie star was having a major hissy fit.

"Not my director, not Thelma Taylor, not

anyone!" Jake declared, standing up suddenly and scraping his chair back.

Snatching the make-up cape from his shoulders, the actor strode out into the corridor, almost stepping on Buster, who darted out of his way. "Call security. Get rid of this bunch!" he yelled over his shoulder.

He was so busy being bad-tempered that he didn't notice Zak turn the corner and run towards him until it was too late.

"You've got to talk to me, like it or not!" Zak pushed Jake against the wall.

"Not now," Jake muttered. "Later!"

"Now!" Zak insisted. He was in a cold sweat, demanding to be heard. "You can't walk away and leave me with the ca… with the problem. That wasn't the deal!"

"Back off, Zak!" Jake warned, aware that nosey parkers Lauren and Megan were still hanging around and that Caitlin and Gemma had suddenly appeared. "You keep your mouth

shut, you hear!"

"And what if I don't?" Zak demanded, more and more desperate as Jake wrenched himself free and began to walk away. He finally snapped, throwing himself at Jake from behind.

Jake turned and swung a punch, missing Zak, who ducked just in time. "What do I care what you do with the stupid cat?" he yelled. "Dump it! Drown it! Do whatever you want –

just don't talk to me!"

The make-up girl had already called Security. Four guards came running, but instead of escorting the girls from the building, they grabbed Jake and Zak and pinned them against the wall.

"Get your hands off me!" the great star yelled. "Don't you know who I am?"

Zak said nothing as the guards dragged him to his feet and prodded him towards the lift.

"What do we do now?" Gemma gasped, watching the lift doors close on Jake and Zak. "We can't spy on them now that the Security guys have grabbed them. And the truth is – we're no closer to finding Jasmine!"

"Want to bet?" Caitlin said. She pointed to the three pups racing back the way she and Gemma had just come. "Go, pups!" she cried.

Dylan, Buster and Daisy didn't hesitate. They raced downstairs, back to the basement car park and in through the entrance of Central Fitness Club. "Yip! Yap! Woof!" They were hot on the trail, calling for the girls to follow.

"Hey, you can't go in there!" A receptionist had spotted them.

Lauren hurried everyone along the corridor after the pups. They headed straight for the men's changing-room, barking as they ran.

Dylan's amazing sense of smell led them straight to a locker in the corner. "Yap!" he said, jumping up at the door.

Megan put her ear to the metal door and listened.

"Miaow!"

It was exactly what she expected to hear! "Well done, Dylan! Over here!" she called to the others.

"Miaow!" Another tiny, muffled cry came from inside the locker.

"The door's locked!" Megan gasped. "But I bet the receptionist has a key."

So Lauren ran to fetch the girl on the desk. "The missing movie cat - Jasmine - she's in here!" she gabbled.

The receptionist followed Lauren and Gemma begged her to open the locker. "Quick – Jasmine's in there – she might suffocate!"

"Miaow!" Jasmine cried from inside.

The receptionist's key turned in the lock. Gemma opened the door to find a lightweight rucksack. She lifted it out and quickly unzipped it.

"Yip!" The puppies yelped a greeting to Jasmine the missing superstar.

Jasmine poked her nose out of the bag and spied Dylan, Daisy and Buster. "Sssss!" she hissed. *Eww, puppies - get them away from me!*

CHAPTER ELEVEN

Prr-prrr! Jasmine nestled in Gemma's arms, ignoring the shock waves that ran through the Mercury building when she carried the missing cat back in.

"I'm so happy!" Gemma murmured, putting her cheek against Jasmine's soft, warm fur. She'd gathered with the crowd outside Thelma Taylor's ground floor office. "You're safe. That's all that matters."

"Call the TV stations! Tell the press that Jasmine has been found alive and well!" Assistants ran along corridors. Actors and production staff burst out of studios to hear the latest news.

"It makes me laugh," Lauren told Megan and Caitlin. "Our magic pups spend all day super-sleuthing to find Jasmine and all she does is hiss at them!"

"Never mind – they did a great job!" Megan knelt and stroked Dylan. "You three saved Jasmine's life."

Dylan tilted his head to one side, flopping one ear up and one ear down.

"Without you, Jasmine would have been stuck inside that locker for who knows how long," Caitlin murmured to Daisy.

Daisy closed one of her bright eyes and seemed to wink.

Prrrr! Jasmine licked Gemma's hand with her rough pink tongue.

"At least she's glad to see *you!*" Lauren laughed.

"Not as much as I am to see her," Gemma sighed. "Just wait until I tell Mom. She'll be over the moon. And she'll probably want to sign up these three amazing puppies to Animal Allstars right away."

"You hear that, Buster?" With a broad smile, Lauren picked her puppy up. "You could be a movie star like Jasmine!"

"Yap!" he said cheekily.

"But we have other plans in mind," Caitlin and Megan said firmly. "So don't even think about it!"

"Quiet, everyone, please!" Ryan Cooper appeared at the door of Miss Taylor's office. "Thelma has a couple of things she would like to say."

The powerful lady soon appeared and the chatter in the lobby stopped. She smiled and beckoned over the girls and their pups. "Here at Mercury we are all so grateful to these brave kids," she announced.

Megan, Lauren and Caitlin blushed bright red.

"And of course to their amazing puppies!" Thelma continued.

"Yip! Yap! Yap!" Looking perky and pleased, Dylan, Buster and Daisy enjoyed the applause.

"We're also delighted to have Jasmine back," Thelma said. "Sure, we could have gone on filming without her, but we would all have missed her and felt that the movie could never be quite the same."

"Miaow!" Jasmine said, as if on cue.

Thelma smiled. "As it is, the kidnap story has been great extra publicity for the movie, so we thank Jake Wood for that and move on."

"Where's Jake now?" someone asked. "What happened to him?"

"The police are interviewing him as we speak," Miss Taylor explained. "They also plan to charge both Zak and Jake with kidnapping poor Jasmine. And I might as well tell you now that I've decided to cancel Jake's contract with Mercury and bring in a new actor to play *Billy the Kid.*"

There was a gasp of surprise, then another round of applause. That was it – Jake Wood was history, and it served him right.

"So thank you again, and now let's get back to work!" Thelma Taylor concluded. "Let's get out there and make *Candy 2* the biggest blockbuster the movie world has ever known!"

"It's weird to be k 🦴 the park," Caitlin said, looking around at the lake and the café. "It feels like nothing happened."

Joggers still jogged, kids still queued for ice cream. Even the old lady was still sitting on a bench reading her book.

"Not to me, it doesn't." Lauren sat down on the grass with Buster on her lap. "I need a rest!"

Megan hugged Dylan and sat beside Caitlin and Lauren. "I'm glad it turned out well for Gemma, even if she couldn't understand why we wouldn't go back to Animal Allstars with her and Candy."

"Well, we had to say goodbye," Lauren argued. "It's been a busy day and it's time for us to go home. Hey, Buster?"

Her hyper pup had just dashed off and got tangled up between the legs of another jogger.

"Come back!" Lauren yelled.

Her puppy ran in a big curve across the grass, returning at last.

"Ready?" Caitlin asked. She stroked Daisy, who gave a tiny yip.

"Ready?" Megan checked with Dylan, Lauren and Buster.

Everyone sat quietly on the grass in the middle of Sleuth City Park.

Then Caitlin, Megan and Lauren leaned forward and gently lifted the gold medallions from around their puppies' necks.

"Don't you just love that floaty feeling?" Lauren sighed, looking round Megan's garden. "And that whizzing around and the bright light. Totally magic!"

"I still feel a bit dizzy," Megan confessed. She watched Dylan and Buster romp up the lawn towards the house.

Caitlin picked Daisy up and tucked her under her arm. "I have to go – I told Mum I wouldn't be late," she muttered.

Megan and Lauren walked with her to the gate. "She'll be wondering if you want to go back to the Magic Mountain Rescue Centre," Megan realised.

"Hey yes, what do you think?" Lauren said. She asked the big question straight out. "Will you choose a rescue pup, or not?"

Pursing her lips, Caitlin glanced down at Daisy.

The silky toy puppy stared blankly ahead.

"No, I'll stick with Daisy," Caitlin said at last. "I've decided – she's magic and she really is the only dog for me!"

Mystery Pups

This card certifies that

H Halley Martin

is a member of the

Magic Mountain Puppy Club

with his/her puppy

Dip Stick

Photo Here